For Devadasi

Suggested for readers ages 5 and up.

Warner Juvenile Books Edition
First American Edition
Copyright © 1988 Jez Alborough
All rights reserved.
This Warner Juvenile Books edition is published
by arrangement with Walker Books Ltd., London

Warner Early Reader™ is a trademark of Warner Books, Inc.

Warner Books, Inc.,
666 Fifth Avenue, New York, NY 10103

 A Warner Communications Company

Printed in France
First Warner Juvenile Books Printing: May 1988
10 9 8 7 6 5 4 3 2 1

Library of Congress Cataloging-in-Publication Data
Alborough, Jez.
Esther's trunk.
Summary: When her trunk loses its trumpeting power,
Esther the elephant pays a visit to the doctor.
[1. Elephants—Fiction. 2. Stories in rhyme]
I. Title. PZ8.3.A33Es 1988   [E]   87-13291
ISBN 1-55782-007-4

ESTHER'S TRUNK

poot!

AN ELEPHANTASY BY

Jez Alborough

**WARNER
JUVENILE
BOOKS**

A Warner Communications Company

NEW YORK

Esther felt just like a chump.

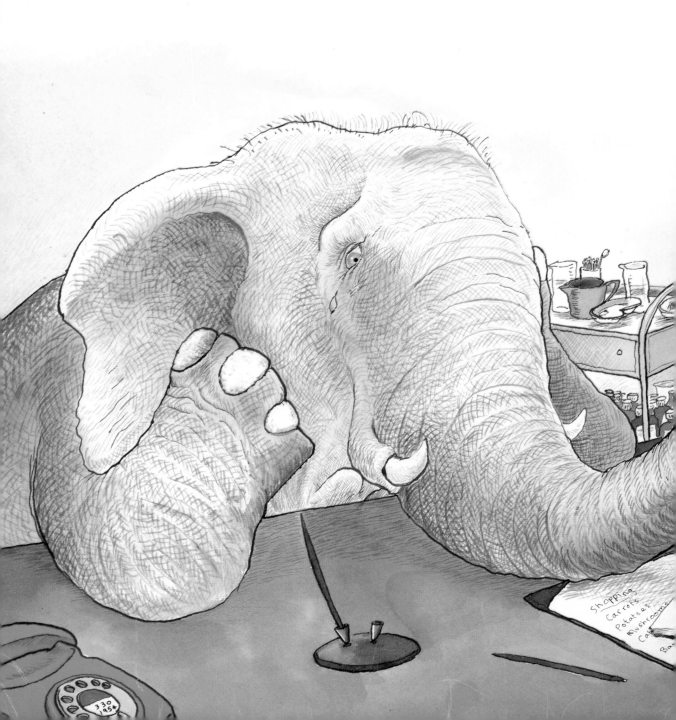

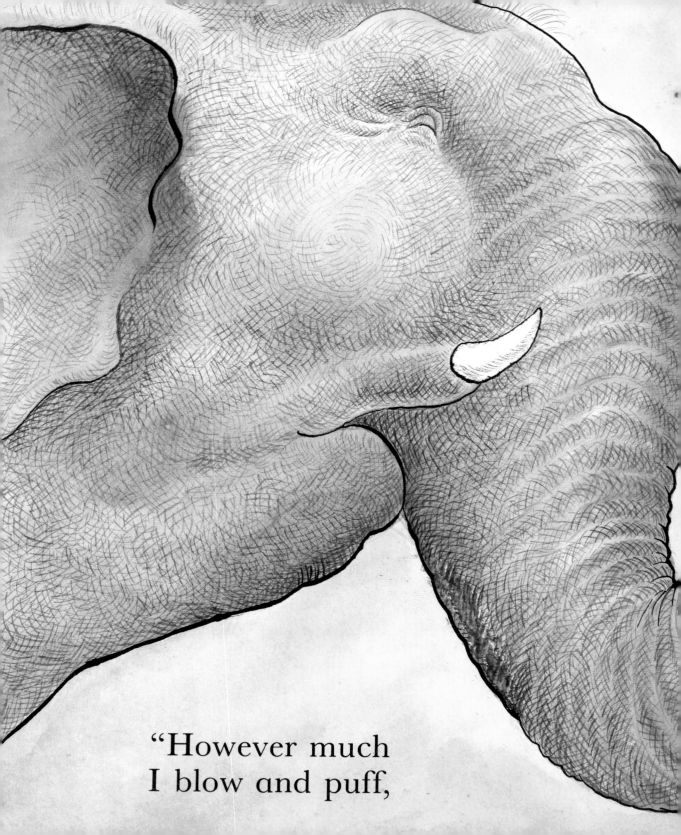

"However much
I blow and puff,

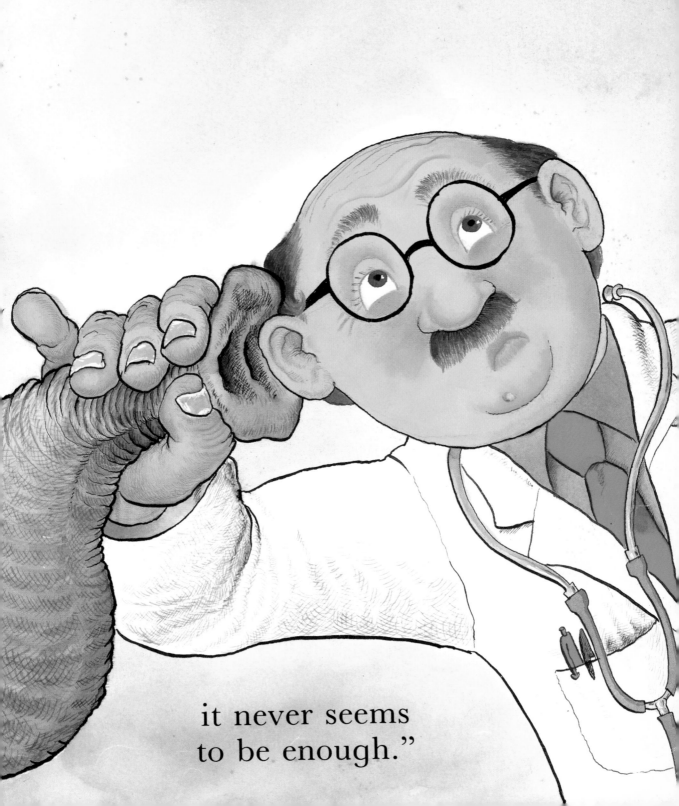

it never seems
to be enough."

The doctor said, "Now open wide
and let me look around inside.

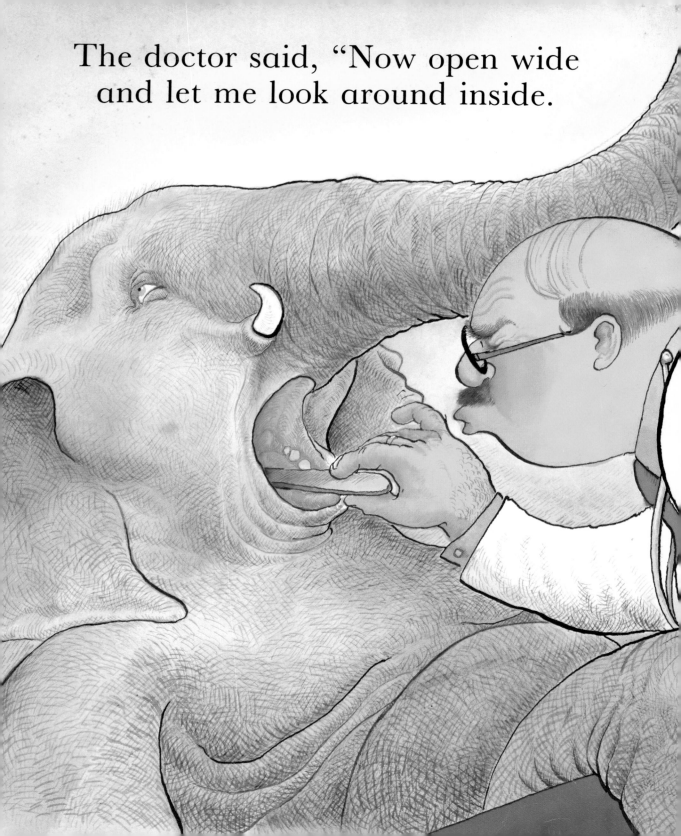

Your throat is fine ...
your tongue seems well ...
but pooh! What is that awful smell?"

"I think I'll try another test.
Just let me listen to your chest.

Both your lungs are clear and strong,
but, my oh my, what *is* that pong?"

Now the doctor has a hunch.
He asks what Esther ate for lunch.

When she answers, "Cheese and pickle,"
he knows the cure ...

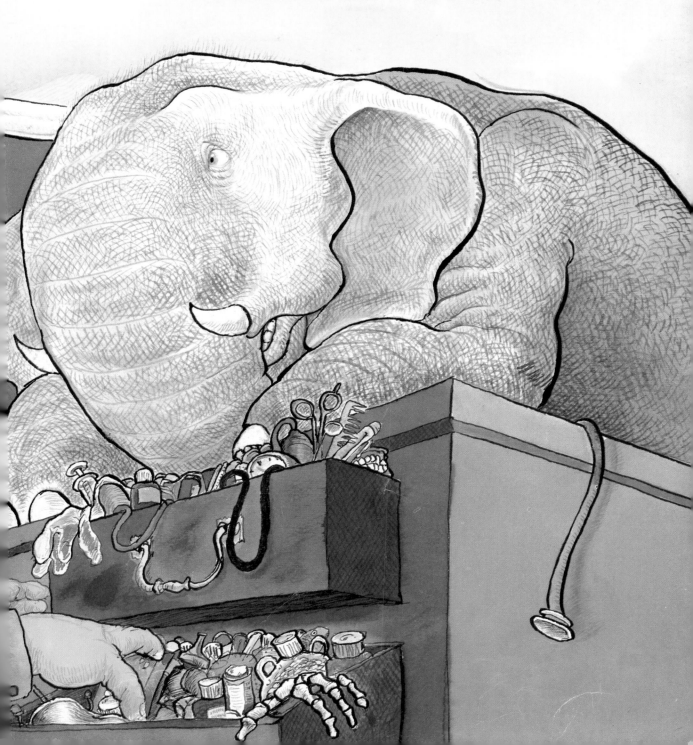

a feather's tickle!

"A … ha …" said Esther, "stop it, *please!*
Be careful or you'll make me sneeze."

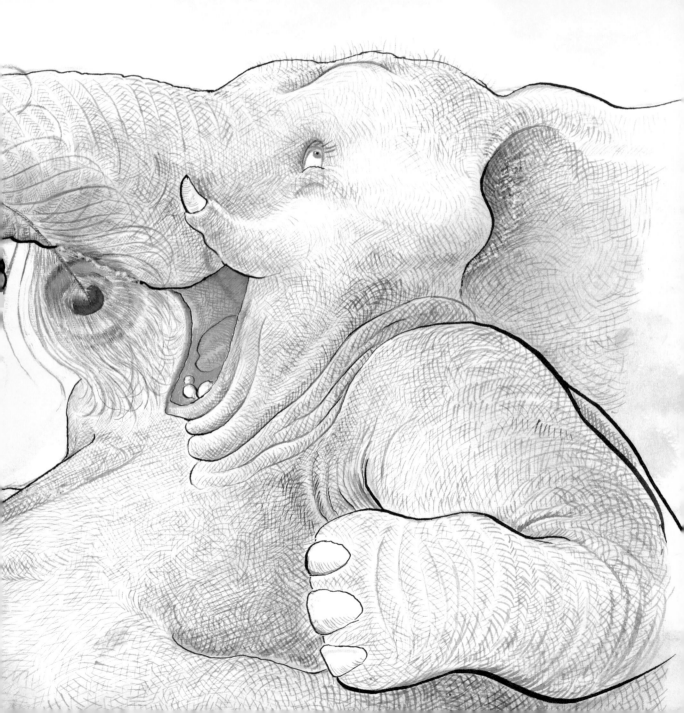

"A ... ha ... a ... ha ... a ... stop it, do ..

aha … aha … aha …   aaaaa …"

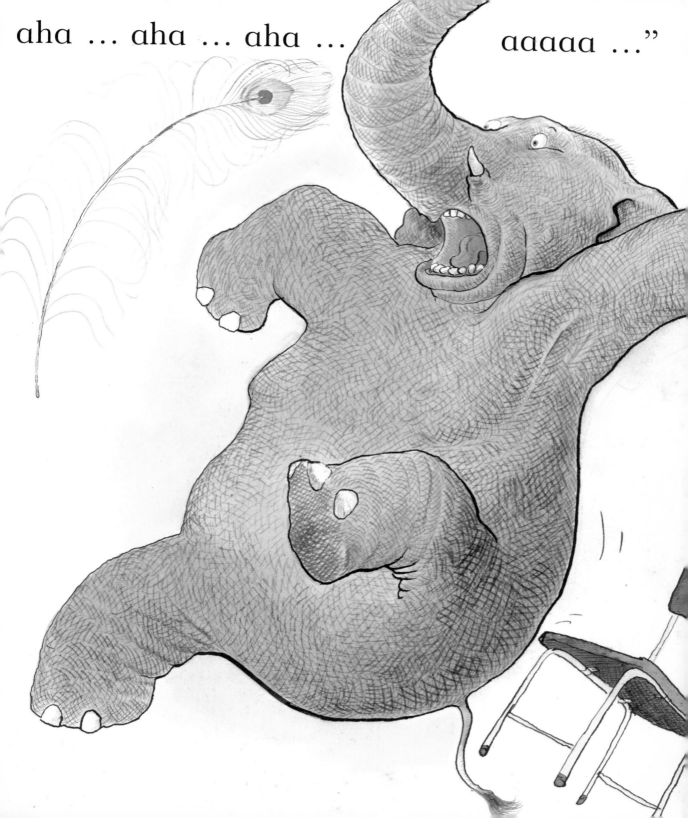

"CHOOOOOO!"

"That's what I smelled!" the doctor cried.

"A tiny pickle stuck inside!"

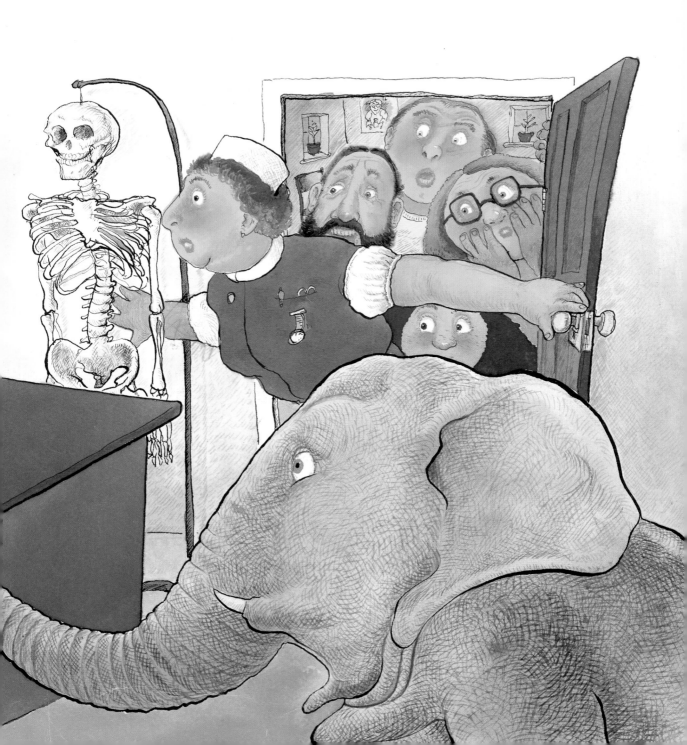

"Now try and blow
without that lump."

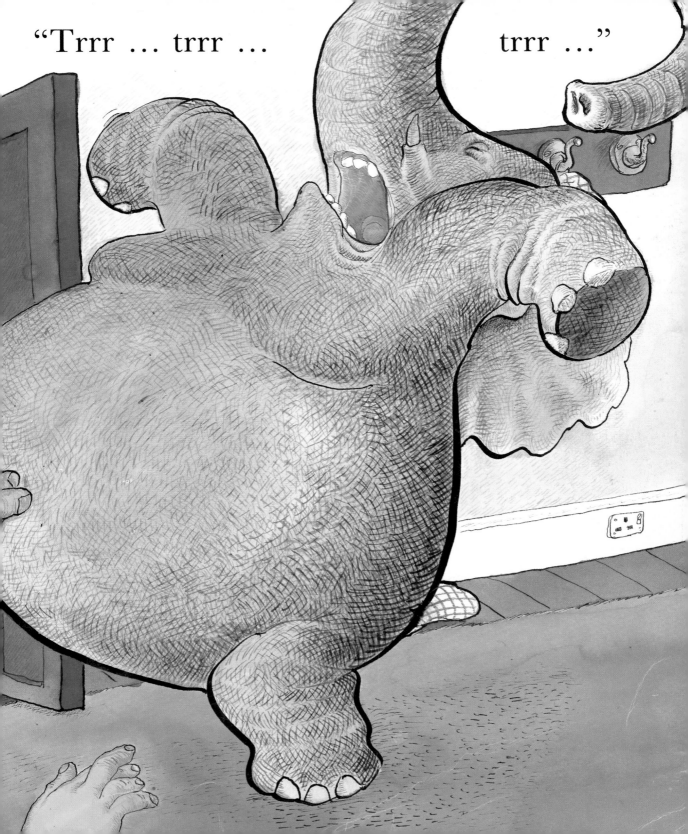

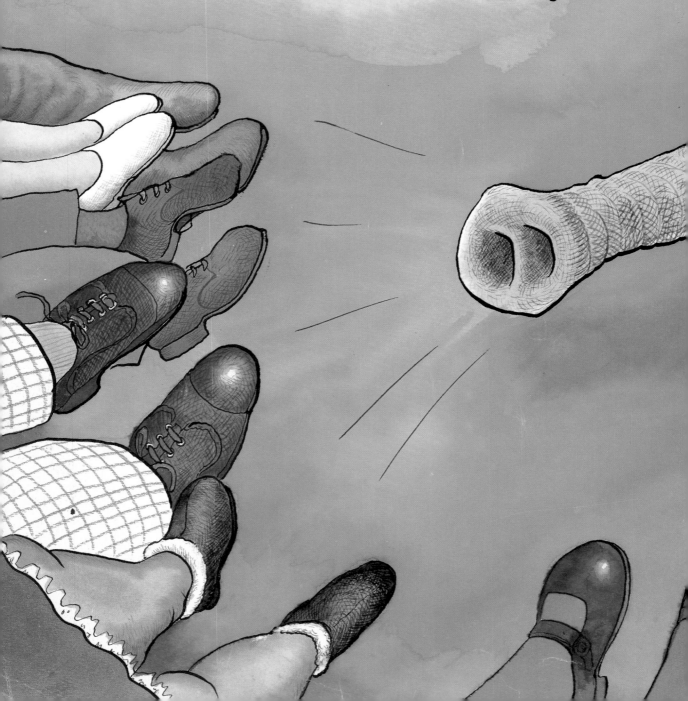

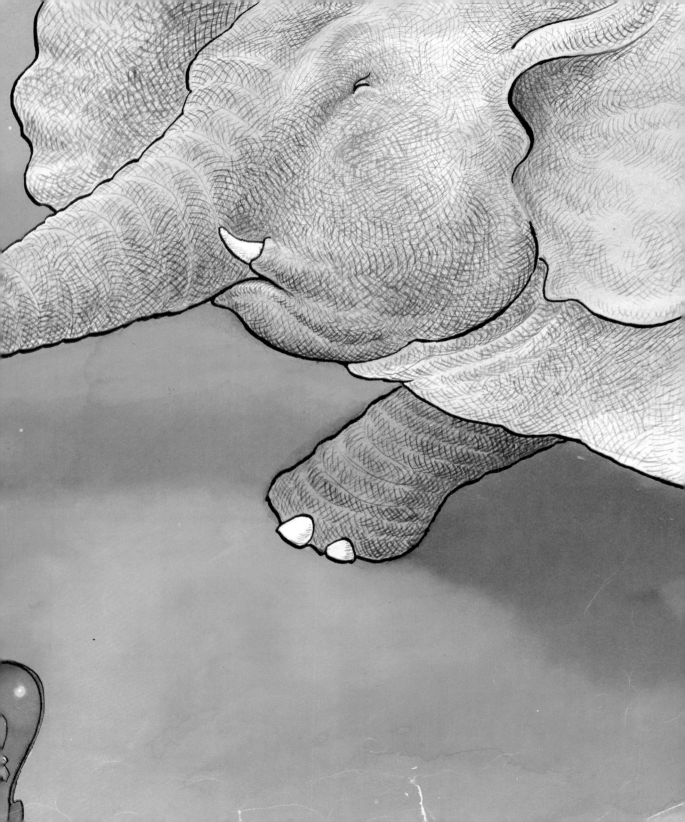

The doctor said, "You see, my dear,
the treatment now is very clear.

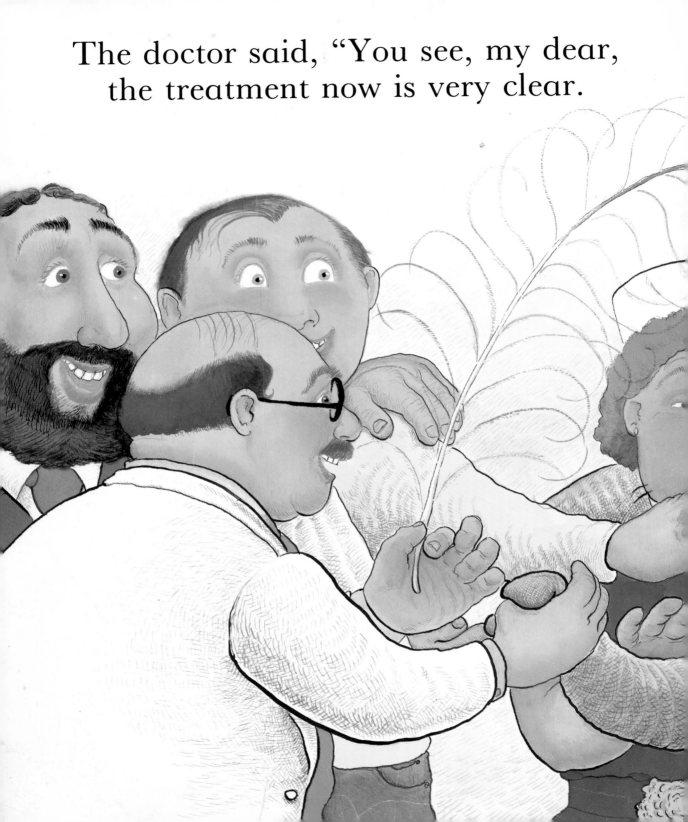

Next time you get in such a pickle,
here's the feather ...
try a tickle!"